I0620969

The Secrets Surrounding Aurora

ISBN

Title page illustration © 05-Bayou-Architecture-Vermilionville-Lafayette-Louisiana-Steve-Chambers-Residential-Architect-Dallas-Architect-acadian-houses-louisiana

Illustration on (p. 4) Hotel Provincial is courtesy of TripAdvisor

(p.9) © depositphotos.com, (p.15) ©https://www.google.com

Illustration on

(p.22)

(p.25)https://www.google.com/url?sa=i&url=https%3A%2F%2Fwww.youtube.com%2Fwatch%3Fv%3DmkmCnvHulng&psig=AOvVaw0XkmH3TUzgAU1HplSBRric&ust=1583807029813000&source=images&cd=vfe&ved=0CAIQjRxqFwoTCLC1rpSrjOgCFQAAAAAdAAAAABAO

p. 27 ©Connecticutbasement

 (p. 55) ©gorgeous-50-note-sankyo-pink-roses-inlay-with-cut-corners-inlay-grand-music-box-50,

To my love, Daniel St. Don, for always having my back and offering input when I can't find the right words.

Hotel Provincial, New Orleans, Louisiana

Chapter One

As I got off the plane from my short trip to New Orleans, Louisiana from Manhattan, New York, I felt like I was on a different planet.

I had been to New Orleans with my family for Mardi Gras when I was sixteen and that trip is what inspired me to major in photojournalism at NYU. I graduated this past May and couldn't wait to return here for the summer.

After I grabbed my carry-on and my bag from baggage claims, I rode a shuttle bus to the car rental place and rented a silver Jeep Cherokee. Then I drove to the Hotel Provincial, near Lake Pontchartrain, where I planned to stay. The place was so much bigger than I pictured it.

Hotel Provincial is a two-story brick building with a black wrought iron gate surrounding the building. On one side, the hotel overlooked a view of the lake. My favorite was the extraordinary black iron fountain in the center, surrounded by a wooden bench.

There were several couples scattered around, either sitting at the tables with a drink or taking pictures.

Once I parked in the lot and received my parking pass, I entered the hotel.

I smiled at the middle-aged woman behind the desk and checked into my room, which would be on the second floor, overlooking Lake Ponchartrain.

I skimmed through the various pamphlets and maps in the magazine rack near the elevators. I thought it was strange that there were no pictures or pamphlets of the Louisiana Bayou.

My room had beige colored walls, oil paintings of flowers and buildings in the French quarter. It's as if within this hotel, the bayous didn't exist. I just shrugged it off.

I called my parents and told them I had arrived safely and promised I would call again soon, as I placed my bags on the bed.

The large windows let in the bright afternoon light, casting shadows of trees blowing in the light breeze outside. I pulled open the long dark brown and beige curtains wider to reveal the sliding glass doors leading to the porch.

I stepped out onto the porch and immediately caught whiffs of Cajun food and the light fresh smells of the flowers blooming on a few of the trees. I was anxious to get outside and explore a bit before eating.

I took my camera from my bag and took a few photos from the porch and then tucked my room card safely into the pocket of my jeans and headed to the elevators.

Once I was back in the lobby, I wandered down the halls and took pictures of the statues. I found the café and captured a few pictures of my picturesque view of the outdoor white iron tables and chairs.

As I walked through the brightly lit café toward the outdoor seating area, I caught sight of a *beautiful* girl. She was sitting on a bench that surrounded the black iron fountain I had seen upon arrival.

She was barefoot with a pair of sandals next to her and her feet were crossed at the ankles. She had long wavy blonde hair, sparkling eyes, and beautifully tanned skin

I raised my camera and secretly took her picture as she tucked a strand of hair behind her ear. She looked happy, yet sad. It made me wonder what her story was.

She departed soon after and headed in the direction of the lake. I sighed and smiled, wondering when and if I would see her again.

After a delicious dinner of Cajun catfish, rice pilaf, and fresh vegetables from a nearby restaurant, I retreated to my second-floor hotel room.

I uploaded the pictures I had taken so far onto my laptop and edited each one carefully.

I paused to gaze at the mysterious girl I had captured. I wondered again what it was about her that made her seem so captivating.

I sat on the porch and propped my feet up on the railing. I enjoyed the sunset, as I captured it with my camera. Then I placed it on my lap and closed my eyes.

The warm breeze around me filled the room with the smells of jambalaya, quiet sounds of laughter, and talking. I heard low humming and smiled. I opened my eyes as the humming got louder and then faded. I stood up to lean on the railing and gazed toward the lake.

I saw the mysterious girl again and quickly grabbed my camera. I captured her with her hair blowing in the breeze. She was now wearing a long turquoise cardigan over her white shorts and purple t-shirt. She dug her bare feet into the sand as she pulled her blonde hair into a ponytail.

Then she slipped her sandals on and headed farther down the beach, out of sight. I sighed and headed back into the room.

I watched T.V. for a couple hours before going to bed. I fell asleep in the bed shortly after, with the patio doors cracked open to let in the light warm breeze.

I woke up around one in the morning to the same humming I had heard earlier and faint crying. I stepped onto the patio and thought I was dreaming. I saw a girl with long dark hair blowing in the breeze. She was wearing a dirty white dress and was barefoot.

The girl seemed to walk with such grace near the lake; it was as if she was floating. I couldn't take my eyes off her. *Was she the ghost of Audrey Teller?!* I wondered.

The disappearance of Audrey Teller was one of the greatest unsolved mysteries in New Orleans. Audrey was said to have disappeared from home at seventeen years old, never to be seen again. Some people say that she drowned in the bayou, but a body was never found. Others say that she left New Orleans and changed her name.

I sighed as I went back to bed and fell into a deep sleep.
I woke up some time later to the bright morning sun. The clock on the end table read 7:45 am. I checked the local weather and it promised to be a beautiful day at 83 degrees.

I yawned and stretched as I pulled myself out of bed. Then I showered, dressed, and slipped into my black flip-flops.

I swiped my dirty blonde hair off my forehead and headed to the café for breakfast, with my camera in hand.
I chose to eat from the buffet, which included fresh baked muffins and breads, strawberries, melon, fritters, and a few french pastries.

After I filled my plate with an apple crumb muffin, strawberries, and a cup of vanilla yogurt, I looked around for a place to sit. The tables inside the café were filled so I went to the outdoor seating area.

I noticed the mysterious girl sitting at a table at the far end. I watched for a moment as she braided her hair into a ponytail. Then I took a deep breath and let it out before approaching her table.

"Hello. Do you mind if I share your table?" I asked as politely as possible.

She looked up at me with her big sparkling blue green eyes and smiled.

"I'm actually waiting for my boyfriend," she said.

"Oh, ok," I said and turned away, feeling a little embarrassed.

"I'm *kidding. Sit. Please,*" she laughed. I sat down and eyed her plate for a moment. She was picking the tiny seeds from her strawberries and munching on chex cereal.

"Why are you doing that? The seeds aren't poisonous," I grinned out of curiosity.

"I know. It's kind of a nervous habit I guess," she said, as she popped the strawberry into her mouth.

"Did you know that the strawberry is the state fruit of Louisiana?" she asked, as she pulled the leaf from another strawberry.

"Yes, I did. I've done my research," I smiled, feeling amused by her.

"I see by the camera that you must be a tourist. Where are you from?" she asked.
"I'm from Manhattan, New York. What about you?" I asked, wondering if she might just be a bored tourist.

"You're looking at it," she said, waving her arm gracefully at the air.

"Well, I'll assume you weren't born here, because you don't have an accent."

"I was born here, but we moved away when I was little and moved back."

"Oh, I get it."

"Yes, well I really *must* go," she smiled in a creole accent as she disappeared toward the lake.

I just shook my head and smiled, wondering where she was going.

Chapter two

Later that day as I went swimming in the lake, I saw the mysterious girl sitting on the sand, a few feet from where my folding chair was. She had dark sunglasses on, so I wasn't sure if she was looking in my direction or not.

She was wearing a striped tank top and white shorts with her hair pulled back. She had her legs bent up and was resting her hands and chin on her knees, while she dug her toes into the sand.

As I got out of the water, I wiped my face with my hands. She smiled as I got closer and I smiled back.

Then I dried my face with the towel and sat in my chair.

"Hey stalker," she smiled, still looking out across the lake.

"Hey, and the name is Noah," I grinned.

"Noah the stalker. It's a catchy name."

"You're *funny*," I snickered.

"My name is Rory by the way."

"Is it short for something?' I asked, curiously.

"Aurora," she said, as she wrinkled up her nose.

"You don't like your name?"

"No, it reminds me of sleeping beauty, you know, the Disney princess."

"So, you're a princess and I'm a stalker?" I joked.

She laughed.

"Did you come here alone?" she asked.

"Yes, I did. I take it you're here with your boyfriend," I said.

She grinned and took off her sunglasses as she bit on the end of them.

"Are you interested in seeing the Bayou?" she asked, squinting from the sun.

"Yes, I am. I was a little disappointed that there were no pamphlets or pictures in the hotel."

"My parents own the hotel. They won't come out to the lake and it's like they pretend the bayou doesn't exist," she said, sadly.

I wasn't sure how to respond.

"I can show you Bayou St. John if you'd like. I have a house there," she smiled.

"Are you sure that you can trust me? I *am* a stalker after all," I smiled.

"My grandmother taught me to always trust your first impressions of people and don't second guess yourself."

I slipped on my flip-flops and t-shirt, and then followed her to the far end of the lake. There was a path through the woods leading to the bayou.

It was like night and day. I lifted my camera and took pictures of the enormous cypress trees and scenery around me as she led me further to her house. I even caught pictures of an alligator poking its head out of the swamp.

It was at least a ten-minute walk from any other house and there were plenty of trees and the swamps of the bayou on her property.

The house was built from cypress wood painted gray, red wooden shutters over the windows to protect them from a storm, and stairs leading to the front porch, with two white wicker chairs and a wicker table.

Rory led me closer to the swamp and bent down to pick something up. She handed me a shiny gold locket with a little mud crusted on it.

"I found this a couple days ago a little farther out in the swamp. The chain was caught under a big rock."

"Wow," I smiled, as I inspected it.

There was an engraving on the back, with the initial A.T. and an engraving of a rose on the front. I popped it open and there was a tiny black and white picture of a girl with dark hair. I gasped, looking over at Rory.

She raised her eyebrows.

"That was my reaction too," she said.

"Did this belong to Audrey Teller?!" I asked, in disbelief.

"I think so. You know the stories?"

"Yes, I do. She disappeared over one hundred fifty years ago though! *How* is this in such good condition?!"

"Well, it's real gold, which doesn't rust in water."

"You should keep this safe," I said, handing it to her.

She raised her hands in defense.

"No way, my grandmother also believed that if you took from the dead, they would haunt you. Well, maybe not in those *exact* words, but still."

"Yes, but you would be *protecting* it. There's no harm in that, right?"

"I don't know. It makes me feel a little uneasy," she said, backing away.

"Well, I'll hold onto it then," I said, putting it in my pocket.

"Suit yourself," she said, as she led me back to her house.

She unlocked the door and the smell of jambalaya filled the air. She stepped up to the counter and took the cover off the crock-pot to stir it around a bit, before covering it again.

"That smells *amazing*," I smiled.

"Thanks. My grandmother taught me how to make it," she smiled.

"You talk about your grandmother a lot. You must be very close."

"We *were*," she said, as she swiped a tear away quickly and smiled.

The house was old, and I was told that the china cabinets and built in shelves were the original part of the house.

"So, was this house passed down through your family line?" I asked, curiously.

"Yes. Well, it was abandoned for about six years or so at one time, but only family has lived here. It's been fixed up a couple times since my grandparents owned it. I know the roof needs to be replaced, because it leaks when it rains," she explained, pointing to the stains on the ceiling.

"I take it you don't have the money to fix it up."

"No, not really. My parents refuse to help. They think the house should be torn down," she said sadly.

In the hall leading to the bedrooms was a padlocked door.

"What's behind this door?" I asked.

"That leads to the dark and creepy basement. I've *never* been in there. They're usually dark, musty, and full of spiders."

"Ah, you're not a spider lover, huh?" I grinned.

She shuddered, and I laughed, as she led me to the other rooms.

There were two bedrooms, Aurora's bedroom, and a guest room. The guest room had a full-size bed made up with white sheets, a homemade quilt, and three pillows. There was a nightstand with a lamp, a matching dresser, and a small bookshelf, which was empty. The top of the dresser had a couple candles on it.

"This house is great. I mean it needs some work, but it is *quite* beautiful," I smiled, as we headed back to the living room.

She pulled open the long curtains to reveal a sliding glass door that went out to the back porch. It was a little smaller than the front porch but had a porch swing.

We sat down on the porch swing and she propped her feet up on the railing, then turned to me and stuck her tongue out as I took her picture.

"I'm going to *assume* you don't have a girlfriend," she said.

"She broke up with me a few months ago," I replied.

"Wow, you really *are* a stalker," she joked, when she saw the pictures that I took of her.

"I think the pictures I took of you are beautiful," I replied.

"*All* of your pictures are *beautiful*. You're like a *professional*."

"I graduated at NYU with a degree in photojournalism," I grinned.

"Really?" she smiled, looking over at me.

I shook my head yes proudly and smiled.

Chapter three

As I woke up the next morning in my hotel room, I just lay there. I had had the scariest dream…

I dreamt that a dark shadow of a person was on the porch, watching me. I kept checking to see who it was and each time it was nothing. After I checked for the third time, I woke up with a rush of terror going through me.

My cell rang suddenly, and I was so startled, I almost fell off the bed.

"Hello," I said, as I gulped.

"Noah. I had the *scariest* dream. I barely slept," Rory said, her voice sounding shaky.

"I had a freaky dream too. What was yours about?" I asked.

"Can you just come over? Can you find your own way here?"

"Yeah, I'll be there soon."

"Thank you and don't forget the locket," she reminded me.

I put the locket in my jeans pocket and headed straight to Rory's house. I almost slipped and fell a couple times.

By the time I reached her porch, I was panting.

"Are you ok?!" she asked, as she pulled me inside.

"I walked here fast, because I had this overwhelming feeling like I was being watched and followed," I said, as I sat at the kitchen table with her.

"So, you first," she said, drinking orange juice.

I explained how I had been filled with fear and woken up in a panic.

"Wow, I'm sorry. I had a nightmare that a black shadow person was watching me from outside. I got up to look out the window and the shadow seemed to get closer and closer until it came right through my window. I woke up screaming and crying."

"Yikes, that's scary. You know, maybe our nightmares had something to do with this locket," I said, setting it down on the table between us.

She picked it up and examined it more closely, scratching the dirt off with her fingernails.

"Maybe. So, what do we do?" she asked, setting it back on the table.

"Well, we're sure that this is Audrey's locket. Maybe we should do some exploring. Maybe your grandmother did some research."

"Where should we start?" she asked.

"The place you fear," I said, raising my eyebrows.

"In the basement?" she asked, scrunching up her nose.

"Yes. I'm here, so you have nothing to worry about."

She sighed loudly.

"Ok, but breakfast first," she replied.

She placed a piece of banana bread on a plate for me.

"Mmm," I smiled, taking a bite.

"I made it at like six thirty this morning," she smiled back.

We finished eating and she found the keys to the padlock in one of the junk drawers. I opened the door and felt around for the switch on the wall.

Door from outside, leading to basement

The light brightened up the dark basement. I squeezed Rory's hand and we started down the stairs slowly. I swiped spider webs away with a broom and we both coughed as dust fell from the rafters.

There was an old unusable washer and dryer to the left of the stairs, a small sink, and boxes stacked up in the corner.

Rory followed close behind as we explored to the right of the stairs. There was a box of blankets covering a wooden hatch with a broken lock. Rory and I raised our eyebrows at each other. I lifted the door to find a set of wooden stairs and darkness.

"What is it?" she asked.

"I think it's a sub-basement," I said, as I used the flashlight on my cell and shined it down the stairs.

Rory followed me down the stairs and soon we were standing in a small dirt room. She shuddered and rushed back up the stairs. I followed close behind and shut the door again.

"I felt *very* uneasy down there," she commented.

"I did too," I replied.

Basement

Sub-basement

"Hey, there's a locked door here," she said, pulling on the handle.

"It must be locked from the outside. Probably a way to get in and out of the basement without going through the house," I guessed.

"Hmm, that's pretty smart," she said.

"We should bring these boxes upstairs to look at," Rory suggested, as she picked up a box from the stack near the washer.

"I agree," I smiled, as I grabbed a couple boxes and followed her back to the living room.

She made us both a cup of coffee as we started carefully going through one box at a time, tossing old bills and shopping ads in a trash bag.

"No way," I said, as I sat down on the couch with an old yellowed newspaper article.

She sat next to me and we looked at it together. The date read, July 15, 1865. The paper was fragile and crinkly, like it would turn to dust in my hands.

"Teller family is torn over the sudden disappearance of their oldest daughter, 17-year old Audrey Teller," we both read aloud together.

We looked at each other in awe and Rory read on further.

"Audrey's father, Ronald Teller said, 'She was a good girl. She wouldn't have run away. I don't know where she is, but we'll continue to look for her,' he told police.

When asked when he first noticed she was gone, he said that she went to bed on the night of July 10 and was nowhere to be found the next morning. The basement door to the outside was closed, but not locked. It was suspicious, but not uncommon.

Police searched the bayou and woods but found nothing unusual.

We were both in shock.

"Oh my god!" she suddenly gasped, as she stood up and covered her mouth, "I think Audrey and her family actually *lived* in this house! That would explain a lot," she said, as she started pacing the floor.

"Well, when was this house built?" I asked.

"I don't know, but it's been in the family for *years,*" she said, "Does this mean I could be *related* to her in some way?!" she asked, as her hands shook, and she continued pacing.

I stood up and stepped in front of her to stop her from pacing. She rested her head on my shoulder and I wrapped my arms around her. She did the same.

"I think we should take a break for a little while. Why don't we go sit out on the back porch for fresh air?"

She agreed, and I led her by the hand to the porch swing outside as she took a couple deep breaths and relaxed.

Chapter four

I woke up in a cold sweat. I looked around, confused, and suddenly remembered that I had stayed in the guest room at Rory's house last night, because she didn't want to be alone.

I pulled on my white t-shirt and thought I heard something, so I looked out the window. I heard the noise again and stepped closer. I thought I saw someone or something running in the woods. I went out to the porch to look but saw nothing. I heard a girl crying and I went back inside.

I peeked through Rory's slightly open door and she was sleeping. I heard the crying again, but it sounded faint. I walked past the basement door and thought I heard someone going down the stairs.

I was a little freaked out, but more intrigued, as I found the keys in the drawer and unlocked the door. Then I turned the light on and headed down the stairs. The faint crying continued as I looked around. I heard the door open suddenly and I saw someone at the top of the stairs.

I gasped as I backed into the corner.

"Noah are you down here?" asked Rory, as she walked down the stairs.

"You scared the *crap* out of me!" I said, as I approached her, placing my hand over my heart.

"What are you doing?" she asked, as she wrapped her arms around herself.

"I heard crying. At first, I thought it was you, but…"

The crying started again, but more faint. We looked around and saw nothing. Rory suddenly jumped back. She had been standing on the wooden hatch.

"I felt vibrating. It may have been just my imagination though," she said.

I turned on the flashlight of my phone and opened the door to the sub-basement as I walked down the steps and looked around. There was nothing different.

"Oh my god! Get out of there!" she suddenly shouted.

I rushed up the stairs, almost tripping, and shut the door again.

"What did you *see*?!" I asked, as my hands shook.

"I saw that black shadow figure down there. It was standing behind you," she said, as she covered her mouth with her hands.

We both rushed back upstairs, and I locked the door behind us. Neither one of us could go back to sleep after that.

"It could have just been *your* shadow, but it reminded me of the black figure outside the other night."

"What if Audrey didn't *just* disappear?" I wondered aloud, as she curled up in my arms.

"What do you mean?"

"What if someone *killed* her?" I asked.

"It's possible," she sighed.

"Since we're up, do you want to go through more papers?" I asked.

"Yeah, why not," she smiled, as I put a box on the floor in between us.

"A lot of this just looks like receipts and old bills," I said, as I tossed a stack of old opened bills into the trash bag.

We started going through another box and there were a lot of papers with her grandfather's handwriting. They looked like he'd been trying to piece together his family tree.

"He got pretty far in his search. I have this one starting at 1899," I smiled.

We continued searching and Rory found one starting at 1840, she followed the writing down and, on the backside, she found what she was looking for. She read what she found to me.

"Audrey Louise Teller born April 16, 1848, in Louisiana, on Bayou St. John. Missing since July 10, 1865. Death unknown. She was the daughter of Ronald James Teller and Jacqueline Marie Le' Cart. She had a sister, Annie Marie Teller, born June 1, 1851. Annie died on October 3, 1927."

"Oh, check this out, it says this house was fully built on August 3, 1820, by Graham Teller, which would have been Audrey's grandfather. So that makes the house…one hundred ninety-nine years old!" I said.

"So, Audrey disappeared one hundred fifty-four years ago and this house was built by her grandfather," she smiled.

"Ugh, my brain hurts from looking at all these words and numbers," I said, as I rubbed my temples with my fingers and leaned back on the couch.

"Well, it *is* 3:25 in the morning," she yawned.

Chapter five

When I woke up the next morning, I heard faint crying.

"Not again," I whispered as I stood up.

I turned toward the kitchen from the couch and saw Rory sitting at the table with her face in her hands.

"Hey, are you ok?" I asked, as I sat down next to her.

She sniffled, as she wiped her eyes and looked at me.

"Um…well, today is my dad's birthday, so I called him and he blew me off. He said that I'm selfish and I should be proud to come from a family with money," she sobbed, covering her eyes again.

"Rory, there is *nothing wrong* with heading on your own path to do what you want," I said, as I held her.

"Yes, but they're my *parents* and it's *different*! It *really hurts*!" she cried, as she sat up.

"I understand that it *hurts*, but eventually they'll be *proud* of what an *amazing* girl they raised."

I smiled, and she stood up to give me a hug.

"I have to shower and dress for work," she said.

"Ok, I'll make breakfast then," I smiled.

I made us French toast with strawberries and powdered sugar. It was all set up on the table when she came out.

"Careful, I could get used to this," she smiled, as we sat down to eat.

"I could stay a while longer if you want," I suggested.

"Do you want to stay until the end of the summer?" she asked.

I hesitated.

"I'd *love* that. Are you sure?"

"Yes, I like having you around," she smiled.

"Cool, then I'll pick up my stuff later," I smiled.

I kissed her before she left half an hour later.

Once she left, I cleaned up and did the dishes. Then I grabbed the house keys and left to get my stuff and check out of the hotel.

I drove downtown to browse the different stores and take pictures and went grocery shopping for us before driving back to the house.

Once all the groceries were put away, I went through the boxes in the living room. I organized the papers from the family tree into manila envelopes I found and set them on the bookshelf.

In another box that I went through, there was a sealed blank business envelope. I opened it up carefully and gasped. It was a wad of hundred-dollar bills. The note inside the envelope read, *'To My darling Aurora Leigh Thomas. This $2,000 is for you. I want you to know that I love you and I'll always make sure you are taken care of. Love, Grandma Sylvie.'*

I smiled and set it aside. There was another sealed envelope that read *'To Sylvie'* on the front. I opened it and read the letter inside:

Sylvie, you know that we've always been great friends. You are a wonderful person. I want you to know how much my family and I appreciated your kind gesture of helping us after the devastating fire took our home.
You really came through for us with a place to stay for a couple months, food, clothes, and household items.
The only way to repay you for this kindness that I could come up with is that if you ever need repairs done to your house at any time in the future, please give us a call. We will do any repairs for free. We love you.
Love ... Gary Marquis and family.

I was excited about the letter and decided I would call as a surprise to Rory and a man answered on the third ring.

"Hello, Marquis Construction. This is Gary, can I help you?"

"Hi, my name is Noah Chase and I'm a friend of Aurora Thomas; Sylvie Thomas' granddaughter."

"Oh wow… how is Aurora doing?"

"She's good, but a little stressed. She's at work right now. We've been going through papers from the basement and I found a letter from you to Sylvie about doing free work on the house as a favor. Is that still in effect now that Sylvie passed away?"

"Of course. I can't believe that Rory still lives there, but I'm happy. What work does the house need?"

"Well, mainly the roof and the kitchen floor. I was hoping it could be done as a surprise for her."

"Ah, you're a good friend Noah. I can handle that. Listen, I'm actually retired now, but I can come by with my boys and we can check the place out. Are you free in about an hour?" he asked.

"Yeah, I'll be here. Thank you so much."

"Not a problem, see you soon."

There was a knock on the door an hour later and I answered.

"Hi, you must be Noah. I'm Gary," the man smiled, holding out his hand.

I smiled as I shook his hand.

I opened the door wider and stepped aside to let him and his two sons in. Gary had darkly tanned skin, short gray hair, and big blue eyes. I guessed him to be at least 6'2", and he was a bit on the heavy side. He still looked to be in good shape though, considering his age.

His sons introduced themselves as Gary Jr. and Joe. Gary looked like his father and I guessed Joe looked more like his mother, with short brown hair and brown eyes.

I showed them different things I had noticed that needed to be fixed and they spotted a leak in the bathroom also.

"The roof may take the longest to repair, but the rest are just minor repairs. We were here to do repairs about 6 years ago and it looks like everything held up," Gary smiled.

"Great, when could you start?" I asked.

"Well, we'll have to get the shingles for the roof, kitchen floor tiles, and pipes for the bathroom sink. It may take a day or two. We could start on Saturday," he smiled.

"Ok, that sounds good. I'll take Rory out for the day."

"Are you planning on taking her to the Annual Peach Festival?"

"I didn't know about the festival, but that'd be fun."

"Oh, you're not from around here?" he asked, as he sipped the coffee that I offered him.

"No, I'm from Manhattan, New York and I'm here for the summer. I just met Rory maybe a week ago," I smiled.

"Ah, I see. Rory and Sylvie have always had a way with weeding the good people from the bad. She must really trust you," he grinned.

"I haven't given her a reason not to," I smiled.

"Great, did you two find the money in the basement yet?" he asked.

"Um…I found one, with a note," I hesitated, wondering if I was revealing too much.

"*One* envelope? There is a total of *four*," he winked, taking another sip.

"Really?!"

"Yes, Sylvie had me hide them in the basement up on the rafters a few months before she died. She didn't want Rory to know about it until she needed it. The plan was for her to call me. It was in a letter on the top of a shelf in the basement," he explained.

"Well, Rory refused to go down into the basement alone, so she wouldn't have known anything about it."

"I guess the money *and* repairs will be a surprise then," he smiled, as we finished our coffee.

"I rechecked the pipes in the bathroom and I may have the parts at my shop. I could leave now and fix it today," Joe said.

"Yeah, that'd be great. Thank you," I smiled.

Joe left in the truck while Gary, Gary Jr., and I went down to the basement.

He found the letter on a built-in shelf near a door to a room I hadn't noticed before. I made a mental note to check it out later. His son found a ladder and set it up to check the rafters.

He found the other three sealed envelopes and dropped them down. I picked them up and opened each one.

"If I'm right, Sylvie saved a total of $20,000 for her," Gary smiled, as his son climbed down the ladder.

"Oh my god, wow!"

We went back upstairs, and I put all the money together in a manila envelope and sealed it. Joe arrived back another ten minutes later and fixed the leak.

"Well, it was nice meeting you Noah and thank you for the coffee," Gary smiled, as we shook hands.

"Thank you very much for everything. Here's my cell number so we can keep in contact on Saturday while Rory and I are the festival," I smiled, as I handed him a piece of paper.

"I'll text you if anything changes," he smiled.

Chapter six

After I made myself a sandwich for lunch and ate, I headed back down to the basement with the broom and my phone for music. The basement really wasn't all that creepy during the day, I decided.

I tugged at the door handle of the other door and groaned. It was locked. I felt around on the shelf for a key and found one on the top shelf. I unlocked the door and pushed it open. I sneezed as dust swirled around me and then settled on whatever it touched.

It was a small room lined with shelves filled with jars of old coins, bullets, and blue glass. There were metal tins, old jars, and old license plates. There was a metal detector, much like the one my dad owned, leaning against a wooden workbench.

The workbench had a lamp on it, a box of empty jars, a stack of old newspapers, and a stack of metal detecting magazines addressed to Robert G. Thomas, Rory's grandfather.

I found a dusty package of unopened batteries and replaced the ones in the metal detector, grinning as it beeped to life. I set it back down, imagining how exciting it would be to metal detect on the old property.

About an hour later, I heard the kitchen door open and knew Aurora was back.

She looked up for a moment and then looked at me.

"Did you paint over the stains?" she asked.

"No, it was Gary," I smiled.

"Gary? You mean as in my grandmother's *friend* Gary?! How do you know about him?!" she wondered.

"I'll explain in a moment. I have something for you first," I smiled, handing her the manila envelope.

She raised her eyebrows and opened it. Her eyes widened as she dumped the money onto the table.

"*Oh my god!*" she gasped, covering her mouth, as she sat down.

"*Where* did this *come from*?! Did you *rob a bank*?!*"*

I chuckled.

"Gary told me that it was the money that your Grandmother saved for you over the years. It was up on the rafters in the basement."

She covered her mouth with her hands again as they shook. Tears welled in her eyes and rolled down her cheeks.

"Not to make you cry even more, but I found this in one of the boxes I was going through this morning," I smiled, handing her the note from her grandmother.

She read it and smiled.

"There is a total of $20,000 dollars there," I smiled, as she took a couple deep breaths and let them out.

"I feel like I just won the lottery," she laughed, as she wiped tears away.

"Oh. By the way, Gary's son Joe fixed the bathroom leak also," I smiled.

"Good," she smiled, as she put the money back in the envelope.

"One more thing, I was hoping we could have our first official date at the festival on Saturday," I smiled.

"So, we're dating now?" she grinned.

"I was *hoping*…"

"Well, personally, I've *never met* a nicer stalker than you," she smiled, and I laughed, "but you're only here for the summer."

"I know, but I *really* wouldn't mind driving like 20 hours to come see you," I grinned.

"Are you *crazy?!*" she laughed.

"I am a little, yeah," I laughed, "But coming back here would definitely be worth it."

"Well, let's just enjoy time together now and we'll see what happens," she smiled.

"Ok, but is that a yes to the festival?" I smiled.

"Yes," she smiled, as she opened the refrigerator to get a drink.

"Aw, you went shopping too?"

"Yes, I figure I should contribute since I'll be staying here."

She sat down with a can of lemonade and smiled.

"I found another small room down in the basement. It looked like it must've been your Grandfather's man cave."

"Oh, then you must've found the metal detector."

"Yes, I was excited about it too. My dad and I go metal detecting around the parks and lakes in New York," I smiled.

"So, what do you say about Chinese for dinner? My treat," she asked, pulling a $100-dollar bill from the envelope.

"Sounds good," I smiled back.

Chapter seven

Three days later…Annual Peach Festival

After we ate breakfast, we showered and dressed. Rory dressed in a short jean skirt with stitched flowers on it, a white t-shirt with an opening in the back, which revealed a tattoo of a bouquet of purple butterflies.

The tattoo on her left shoulder was angel wings with the initials *S.R.T.* under it.

"So, is S.R.T. your grandmother's initials?" I asked, taking a wild guess.

"It stands for Sylvie and Robert Thomas actually, both of my grandparents," she smiled, "Are you ready to go?"

"Yes," I smiled back as we locked up. I left my copy of the house key underneath the welcome mat for Gary.

I texted Gary once I parked in the lot at the festival. He texted me back and said they'd head to the house in a few minutes. I couldn't thank them enough.

We could hear music and smell Cajun food almost as soon as the signs for the fair came into view. I parked in the lot when we arrived, and we walked around hand in hand. I eyed several tents before we stopped at a tent that was selling fresh strawberries and peaches. Rory paid for a couple peaches and handed me one.

Next, we stopped at a tent with a duck shooting game and I won a small stuffed crocodile for her.

We rode on the teacups, carousel, tilt-a-whirl, and Ferris wheel before stopping to get something to eat. We each had a hot dog and drink and shared fries. As we finished eating, a middle-aged man approached our table.

"We need to talk," he said to Rory as he gave me a dirty look.

I heard shouting from the side of the building and balled my hands into fists as I listened in disbelief. Soon after, I saw him leave and Rory rushed away.

I couldn't *believe* that her dad treated her like that. I let out the breath I was holding and went back to the car. She was leaning against the driver's side of the car, chewing gum with a tear stained face.

I approached her, and she wrapped her arms around me.

I drove us around downtown for a while; to give Gary and his sons time to work at the house. Rory didn't seem to notice or mind at the moment.

"I thought you were driving me home," she said, after several moments of silence.

"I figured we could just drive around for a little while, to cool off. Is that ok?"

"Yeah. I'm sorry about all this. My dad is...*impossible* to please."

"You have *no reason* to be sorry. He has *no* right treating you like that."

"I've dealt with it since I was thirteen. My mom isn't much better sometimes. She's called me a selfish bitch on more than one occasion."

"*Wow*, I *can't imagine* parents talking to their daughter like that," I said, shaking my head in disbelief.

"Well, that's why I chose to live with my grandmother as soon as I graduated high school. People I thought were my friends have called me irresponsible and selfish also. It's impossible to reason with anyone who cares more about money than anything else.

My cell rang just then, and I pulled it from my pocket to answer it.
"Hello," I said.

"Hey, it's Gary. Are you two still at the festival?"

"No, I was driving around. What's up?"

"Well, the roof is fixed, and Joe is laying down the last of the kitchen tiles. We'll only be another half an hour or so if you wanted to head back."

"Ok, sounds good. Thank you so much."

"Of course. We'll see you soon."

"Ok, great. Bye."

"Who was that?" she smiled.

"It was a friend who was helping me with something. Would you like to get some ice cream?"

"Sure," she squinted.

I knew she was curious but didn't say another word.

Chapter eight

As we pulled into the driveway, her face lit up. Gary's truck was there and him and his two sons were sitting on the porch with a beer. After I parked, she rushed up to them and gave each of them a hug.

"Wow, you've really grown into a beautiful young lady," Gary said.

"Thanks," she smiled, "It's so nice seeing you three again."

"I don't think I've seen you this happy since you first moved in here."

"My life has been full of challenges. Noah is a breath of fresh air," she smiled, as she squeezed my hand.

"I'm glad to hear that," he smiled.

She smiled and followed us inside and I thought she was going to cry.

"I *love* the new floor!" she said of the shiny marble white and gray tile in the kitchen.

"How much do we owe you?" she asked Gary.

"Not a thing. We owed your grandmother a favor and it was to fix any repairs to the house while you live here," he smiled.

She hugged him as tears came to her eyes and they left soon after.

"Can you guess what's been on my mind?" she asked.

"Audrey?" I assumed.

"*Yes.* It boggles my mind that no signs of her remain, *except* for that locket."

"Well, we know that she was born here and grew up in this house. Maybe we need to start thinking outside the box."

"What do you mean?"

"We should use the metal detector and do some exploring,' I smiled.

The next afternoon, we headed outside with her grandfather's metal detector. The only things we seemed to be finding were junk. After half an hour, Rory grabbed my wrist and pointed under the house.

We saw a turtle crawl out, followed by six baby turtles. We looked at each other and smiled as the family slowly made their way to the swamp.

I used the metal detector under the house, and it beeped like crazy. We happily crawled under a little ways and uncovered old coins, bb gun shells, and can tabs. As I dug a little deeper, I found a box.

I brushed the dirt off and noticed that it was a wooden music box with flowers on it. I opened it and heard the hauntingly familiar tune as a gold heart twirled around. Rory was startled and bumped her head as she quickly crawled out.

"Are you ok?" I asked, as I crawled out after her.

"Yeah, I recognize that tune though. I tend to hum it when I'm alone. It's in my head and I couldn't figure out where it came from before."

I examined it closer and ran my fingers over a dark spot in the bottom corner. The heart was engraved with the letters ALT.

"Wow," I smiled.

"What?" she asked.

"These are Audrey's initials, so this must've belonged to her."

"Well, they're my initials also," she sighed, as I followed her inside and we sat at the kitchen table, placing the music box between us.

"I wonder who gave it to her," she said aloud, as the pain in her head subsided.

Music box

We went to bed that night and fell into a restless sleep. A few hours later, I awoke to her crying.

"Hey, what's wrong?"

"I have a migraine," she replied, between gasping breaths.

I stumbled tiredly to the bathroom to find pain reliever. I returned with a glass of water and two exedrin. Then I kneeled in front of her and kissed her forehead. As I took the cup from her, she gasped for air.

"Should I call a doctor?" I asked, concerned.

She shook her head no.

She took another sip and dropped the cup, as she choked and coughed up water. Then she curled up and cried.

"*Please* tell me what's happening," I pleaded, close to tears myself.

She squeezed my hand soon after.

"Are you ok?" I asked, as I glanced at the clock on the nightstand…1:47am.

"Yeah, I don't know why that happened, but I'm fine now."

"You're honestly kind of freaking me out."

"*Honestly,* I'm *fine.* I promise," she yawned.

I wasn't convinced but crawled into bed and held her tight.

Chapter nine

"Are you ok from last night?" I asked later the next morning, as I handed her a cup of coffee.

"Yeah, I'm sure. I mean the migraine was sudden. Then when I choked, I felt like I just took in a lot of water. It was an *awful* feeling."

We sat in silence as I picked up the music box and ran my fingers over the dark spot I noticed yesterday.

"What are you thinking?" she asked after a few minutes.

"When you had your migraine, did it feel like you'd been hit over the head?" I asked her.

"I suppose so, yeah."

"Well, maybe Audrey was hit over the head with this," I said, curiously, as I raised my eyebrows.

"So, you think I'm being affected by what may have happened to her and those dark spots might be her *blood?!*" she asked, looking fascinated.

"Well, I'm no forensic expert, but *maybe*."

"Wow, after all this time?!"

"I don't know, *possibly*. All I can do is guess. My guess is that if she *was* killed, it was pretty brutal. Does that scare you?"

"I think I'm more scared that we'll actually *find* something, like a *body*."

"Well, I doubt that'll happen, but we've gotten this far, and you've got to admit that you're intrigued."

She hesitated and then smiled.

"I *am*, considering she's a part of my family history."

We ate breakfast and dressed in old clothes, to go out metal detecting again.

Rory took over this time and metal detected closer to the swamp and woods. She uncovered old coins, bullets, an old butter knife, and a necklace. The necklace was silver and didn't look very old or expensive.

We heard a rustling noise from the woods that startled us, and she stepped back into a small hole. I caught her before she hit her head on a tree behind her.

Inside, Rory sat at the table with the music box. She held it in her hands and closed her eyes.

"Are you…" I started.

"Shhh," she interrupted me.

About five minutes later, she let go of the box and opened her eyes.

"I was hoping to get a sense for Audrey. My grandmother used to be able to communicate with my grandfather after he died by holding something of his."

"I take it that it didn't work then."

"No, nothing. I don't get it. If what I felt last night was maybe her way of communicating what happened, then why not now?"

"Maybe something will happen again tonight."

"Oh, like another migraine and the feeling of choking? I *hope* not!"

"Do you have a Ouija board? We could try to contact her."

"Do you know how *bad* those are?! You can release *evil spirits* with those."

"I thought that was just in the movies."

"No, stuff like that *really* happens. Anyway, if she really wants to be heard, we can just talk to her," she replied, shrugging her shoulders.

"Really? It's that easy?" I asked.

"Well, I have the same gift as my grandmother. If it's strong enough, I can see things. Also, if I concentrate on someone who has crossed hard enough, I can communicate with him or her. Does that freak you out?"

"No. That just makes you *so* much more intriguing," I smiled, as I held out my hands to her across the table.

She took my hands and smiled as we closed our eyes.

"Audrey, if you're here, give us a sign," she said after a couple minutes of silence.

We sat and waited for a moment, listening for any noise or sound that was out of place.

Suddenly we heard a faint noise from the living room and both got up quickly to peek into the living room.

The locket, which had been on the bookshelf, was now on the floor.

"Oh my gosh," Rory gasped, "Did it *really work*?!" she asked in disbelief.

I smiled, and we sat across from each other at the coffee table. Again, we held hands and closed our eyes.

"Audrey, please tell us how you died," she said.

A couple minutes went by and I clearly heard a faint voice say, *"Burn it."*

We opened our eyes and looked at each other.

"Yes, I heard that," she whispered, as her voice shook.

"Burn it," we both heard again.

A few moments later, we heard faint crying and humming. The humming we now realized was definitely the same tune as the music box.

"I think she wants us to burn the music box," I said quietly.

We heard her humming and crying again.

Rory grabbed lighter fluid and matches while I grabbed the music box and an old metal pot. We went out to the small backyard, put the music box in the pot, and set it on fire.

We thought we saw a black shadow appear and then disappear, but neither of us spoke about it.

As we lay in bed that night, we listened to Audrey's faint humming. I woke up hours later to Rory crying next to me.

I glanced at the clock and it read 1:36am.

"Do you have a migraine again?" I asked, as I turned to face her.

"No, she *showed* me what happened to her this time," Rory whispered, as she faced me and reached for my hands.

"What *happened* to her?" I whispered.

"It was *awful*. She went down to the basement and used the side door to get outside. It was sprinkling out and she was wearing a white dress and had bare feet. She walked to the woods, near the swamps and some guy about her age was waiting there for her. They talked for a few minutes and he offered her the music box. She told him it was beautiful, but she couldn't accept it and he was upset. You should have *seen* the look on his face! He hit her hard in the head with it and she fell back onto the ground. When he reached down to grab her, she kicked him away and stood up. As she tried to run, he grabbed her. Her locket came loose and fell off in the struggle. Then he broke her neck before shoving her into the swamp," she cried.

"Wow, that *is awful*," I gulped.

"I *heard* her neck snap, Noah," she shuddered.

"That was *much* more vivid than I thought it would be," I said.

"How did *nobody* find her body?! I *don't understand*!"

"I...I don't know," I stammered. "The swamps can be unforgiving. You said that it had been sprinkling. Maybe it started raining harder after that, which would've made it easier for him to bury the music box and for her body to drift away.

She could've gotten caught on something underwater. There are also crocodiles in the swamps."

She shuddered.

"The thought of crocodiles getting to her is *not* an image I wanted in my head."

"I'm sorry, but there's *so* many possibilities."

"I know. Poor Audrey can't rest until her body is found."

"It's been over a hundred years. There's not much possibility she'll be found now."

"Yes, I know. I feel like the darkness around her is gone though, because we destroyed the music box."

"Well, we should try to get some sleep," I said, as I squeezed her hands.

She kissed me and I held her close as we both drifted off into another restless sleep.

Chapter ten

The next morning, I had the idea to metal detect near the swamp again, more thoroughly. Rory was a bit hesitant, but she followed me to the woods.

There was beeping in several spots, but we only found coins and bottle caps. I held the detector over the water a bit and as I scanned over a large fallen cypress tree, it beeped continuously.

I glanced over at her and she raised her eyebrows. Then I handed her the detector, took off my sneakers, and stepped into the water a bit.

"*Please* be careful," she said.

"The water isn't really flowing right now and it's not that deep," I said, just before my foot sunk into the mud and I slipped.

I caught myself before I fell and went under the murky water. I pulled my foot out of the mud and then blindly felt around to see if there was an opening.

"I found an opening in the tree. Do you have any swim goggles?"

"Yeah, in my bedroom closet. I'll go get them."

She rushed back to the house and came back out soon after. I put the goggles on and crossed my fingers across my chest before carefully finding the opening again.

Then I raised my eyebrows, took a deep breath, and went under. The cypress tree was big enough for me to climb into and crawl around. I came across a piece of cloth and picked it up. It looked like it had once been white. I held onto it tightly and felt around. I saw something shiny and reached for it.

It was a ring, but it was attached to a bony hand. I let out a scream, forgetting for a second that I was still underwater. I started choking and quickly crawled out of the tree and resurfaced, as I gagged and choked.

"Noah, you're *not* supposed to open your mouth," Rory said, as she pulled me out.

I dropped to my knees and coughed up water. It felt like my chest and throat was on fire.

"Are you ok?" she asked, kneeling in front of me.

I grabbed her hand as I wiped my mouth and gasped as I tried to catch my breath.

"I...I...I think I found Audrey," I said, as I opened my other shaky hand and showed her the white cloth I'd been grasping, "I think the gold ring that made the detector beep was still attached to her finger," I managed to say, in a shaky tone as my throat burned.

Her eyes grew wide and she covered her mouth with her hands.

"Wow. So *that's* why her body was never found. It was inside that fallen cypress tree. She was already dead before she was dumped in the swamp, so there was no struggle," she explained.

"Her spirit hung around waiting for her body to be found and for a proper burial. We owe her that much."

"We *need* to call the cops," she said, as she sniffled.

I nodded my head in agreement.

Rory stood up and helped me to my feet and we headed back to the house. We were both still shaken up.

She called the cops and told them what we found. I'm not sure if they believed us, but they said they'd send someone.

I took a shower and changed before a couple cops showed up twenty minutes later. They sat down at the kitchen table to talk to us.

"Ok, explain again how you came across human remains in the swamp," one of the officers said.

I spoke as the other officer wrote things down. I explained what had happened and held out the piece of cloth I had found.

"Hmm. Have you seen anything suspicious recently?"

"This wasn't *recent*. We believe that the bones belong to Audrey Teller," Rory chimed in.

The officers laughed, and we felt offended.

"Audrey Teller is a *myth*. The story of her disappearance is what parents tell their kids to *keep them away* from the swamps," Officer Farmer said.

"No *offense*, but what *planet* are you living on? I live in *New York* and I know the stories. Besides, we have proof that Audrey lived here," I replied, glancing at Rory.

She found the old newspaper article and the page from her family tree to show them.

"No way," they both said, as they looked at the old papers and then at us.

"You're *related* to her?!" Officer Green asked.

"I just found out recently, but yes. My family never talked about her, but I knew the stories like everyone else. She lived here in this house."

"Well, were there any other clues found? We'll need to do an autopsy and the cold case unit will want to investigate."

"I ..." Rory started.

"No, there's nothing else," I interrupted.

"What were you going to say?" Officer Green asked Rory as he glared at me.

She glanced at me and I raised my eyebrows.

"I um…I have the ability to communicate with people who have died."

Officer Farmer chuckled.

"See, *that's* why I interrupted her! Is everything a *joke* to you?!" I shouted, feeling frustrated.

"I don't *appreciate* the tone. I'm sorry if I was being disrespectful though. Go on," he said to Rory.

"Well, she showed me what happened to her while I was sleeping."

Rory repeated the awful dream of Audrey's untimely death, with less emotion to the officers.

"Wow, that sounds terrifying. So, I'll assume that her body was swept into the cypress tree, which is why she was never found. It seems like they didn't do a very thorough investigation back then."

"We can go out there to reinvestigate, so we can retrieve the bones," Officer Green replied.

Rory and I smiled with approval and followed them outside. I showed them the fallen cypress tree where I had found the bones and then let them do their job.

The officers had to call on the Cold Case Unit and the Underwater and Confined Spaces Unit to investigate and retrieve the bones. It was a hectic scene when the teams arrived.

By now, there was a crowd of curious people forming in the yard. There were people from the bayou and tourists from the lake side trying to figure out what was going on. Some were taking pictures. Rory began getting uncomfortable from having so many strangers on her property. I took her by the hand and led her to the porch.

"Are you ok?" I asked, as I pulled her close to me.

"I thought all this would be more private. It's just *really* overwhelming."

"Well, people love a good mystery," I said.

The action was pretty short-lived. Within another half hour, the excitement dissipated, and the people stepped off her property.

Officer Farmer approached us not long after.

"I want to apologize for making light of the situation," he smiled.

"We'll keep in touch with the results," Officer Green promised.

Chapter eleven

A week later, I had to head home. I had an important job interview with Sandbox Studios in New York City.

I got a text from Rory this morning, the day after my interview.

Hi. How did the job interview go?

I got the job! I showed him my portfolio with the pictures from New Orleans and he was impressed. We ended up having a conversation about my time there and he wants me to write a story about it and said he'd publish it!

Oh, Noah, I'm so happy!

He also wants me to head back to New Orleans to do another story.

That's awesome! When?

Soon.

I can't wait.

Have you heard anything about the results?

Officer Green called last night and said that they may have the name of the person who killed her.

Did he give you a name?

No. You'll have to talk to them yourself.

Ok. I'll let you know when I'm headed there.

Ok. I love you Noah.

I love you too Rory.

As I headed into the office today, my boss approached me with a smile. He held out an envelope and I opened it to find a round trip ticket for a week in New Orleans. The flight was for the next morning at 8:30.

"I trust you won't disappoint me," he grinned.

"No, not at all. They found the person who did it, but I'll have to talk with someone to get the full story."

"Great. I want pictures too, if that's possible."

"I'm on it," I smiled.

He patted my shoulder and walked away.

The next morning, as I found my seat on the plane, my mind was on Rory and the adventures that awaited me. I decided that I wouldn't text her until the plane landed at the airport there.

Soon after, I texted her.

Hi. I'm at the airport.

Ok. I'll see you soon.

Can you pick me up? I'm here now, in New Orleans.

Oh... I'll leave now.

See you soon.

Rory rushed to give me a hug as soon as she saw me.

"Welcome back," she smiled.

We spent the day at the beach and then at her house.

"So, I'm kind of surprised they were able to find out who killed her, with so little to go on," I said curiously, as we sipped a beer on the front porch.

"I wish they could have told me something. Do you think the cops will actually tell *you*?" she asked.

"I was hoping to talk to the cops that we spoke to a couple weeks ago. I'll call in the morning and ask about it," I smiled.

The next morning, after we dressed and ate breakfast, I called the New Orleans police station. I was happy to talk to the same cops and one of them agreed to come to the house and discuss what he knew.

Once Officer Green arrived, we sat at the kitchen table and offered him a cup of coffee.

"So, how did you find the person who killed Audrey so quickly?" I asked, with a pen in hand.

"Well, after my partner and I learned that Rory's family was related to Audrey's family through the line, we did some digging of our own. Audrey's younger sister, Annie had a boyfriend at the time, at 14 years old, by the name of Gabe Lewis. Gabe's older brother John Lewis was known to be quite odd and had a crush on Audrey. It turns out that he killed himself a week after Audrey's disappearance," he explained.

"Wow, so that didn't seem *suspicious* to them?" I asked.

"Gabe and John's father, Jacob Lewis was the Sheriff at the time, so it was covered up and the case was dropped."

"My dad's Great Grandfather was Gabe Lewis," Rory announced, with raised eyebrows.

"I guess that might explain why your dad doesn't like the bayou. I mean, if he's aware of the family history at all," I replied.

"I don't know, maybe I'll try to talk to him. Thank you for coming here and telling us all this," Rory smiled at him.

"You're welcome. Thank you for the coffee," he smiled, as we walked him to the door and sat on the porch.

"Wow, my head is *spinning*. This is *crazy*," she said, as she leaned back in the chair.

"So, then Gabe would have been your Grandma Sylvie's Grandfather then, right?" I asked.

"Yes, although his name was never mentioned. I found him in the family tree."

"So, do you know *your* Great Grandparents at all or are they both gone now?"

"I don't know honestly."

"Do you remember if Sylvie had a brother or sister?" I asked.

"No, she didn't. She was an only child, like me. If I want to know anything more, I'd *have* to talk to my dad."

"Dad, I just want to talk," I heard Rory say from the living room the next morning.

She put the cordless on speaker.

He sighed.

"What did you want to talk about?"

"Well, have you heard about Audrey Teller's bones being recovered?"

"Rory...you *know* I don't really watch the news. I *have* heard some of the tourists talking though. I didn't realize so many people were interested in such an old story."

"Well, did you hear that they were found in Bayou Saint John, by Noah and me?"

Silence.

"Um…*excuse* me?! How in the *hell* did you find something like that?!"

"I'll let Noah tell you. He's right here."

"Hello Mr. Thomas."

"*Please* explain what's going on."

"Of course. A couple weeks ago, Rory and I were metal detecting near the swamp on her property and it beeped over a fallen cypress tree. I explored and found a ring attached to a bony hand, along with a piece of white cloth. We called the cops and they did an investigation. The bones belonged to Audrey Teller."

"Oh. My. God! So, the tales are true?! Her ghost really walks the bayou?"

"Yes. I've seen her myself and so has Rory."

"So, did she really live in that house that Rory lives in now?"

"Yes dad. Her younger sister Annie was married to Gabe Lewis, your Great Grandfather," she replied.

"I heard that his brother hung himself in their barn when he was 19."

"John is the one who killed Audrey a week before he killed himself."

"I…I didn't know that."

"I thought you knew the history just a *little* and that's why you wanted nothing to do with the bayou."

"No…that's really what you *thought?*"

"Yeah…you always just told me it was dangerous, without an explanation."

"Rory, you saw two kids *drown* in the bayou when you were just five years old. That's the reason we *moved.* It was *traumatic* for all of us. We moved back to New Orleans when you were thirteen. You *really* don't remember?"

"No, I don't. Grandma Sylvie never told me anything either."

"I made her promise not to bring it up. I honestly didn't know that much about our family history. It is interesting to say the least."

"Can we start over? I miss you and mom."

"I'd like that. I'm *so* sorry I've shut you out. I should have just told you the truth, but you're *so stubborn.*"

"I get my stubbornness from you," she smiled.

"I love you, darling."

"I love you too, dad."

This is a fictional story, although Bayou St. John, Lake Pontchartrain, and the Hotel Provincial are really in New Orleans, Louisiana.

www.ingramcontent.com/pod-product-compliance
Lightning Source LLC
Chambersburg PA
CBHW020334130626
46549CB00003B/1178